Mermaid Kenzie
Protector of the Deeps

WITHDRAWN

Charlotte Watson Sherman

illustrated by Geneva Bowers

BOYDS MILLS PRESS

AN IMPRINT OF ASTRA BOOKS FOR YOUNG READERS

New York

"McKenzie!"
Mama mad. Again.

Everybody know
my name is *Mermaid* Kenzie.
Protector of the Deeps.

"Mussy McKenzie," Mama say. "Clean up before beach."

"Mermaids don't clean up."

"Oh?" Mama say. "Then this mermaid don't go to the beach."

"But—"

Beach Day!
Stones to skip.
Sand to castle.
Sunbleached sticks to dig for treasure.
Seashells buried in golden sand.
Shark teeth!
A stream to cross
holding Mama's hand
till I run off and ramble through the giant cave
that echo echo echoes.

Sometime we see a pelican parade.

At night,
lantern fish swim up from the deep,
a festival of blue light.

"Higgledy-piggledy," I say
and attack the monstrous mound
of mussy
downside-up inside-out
jumbled stuff.

Finally, the wavy dune.
"Hurry, Mama!"
Sea waves whispering
our favorite watery tune.

Mist silver the water,
briny taste on our tongue.
Seaweed perfume the air.
Gray, the heron, drift past,
wing almost blocking the sun.

The high arch of the cave calls,
I poke pockets of shadow,
then an earthy shock—
a whiff of worm in my nose
and wet rock.

I skedaddle.
Wind whistle in my ear
till I brake at the rocky edge of the glittering sea
where—*abracadabra*—waves turn into foam
licking me.

A tide pool waits.
And a drop of squirmy water
to study with my microscope.

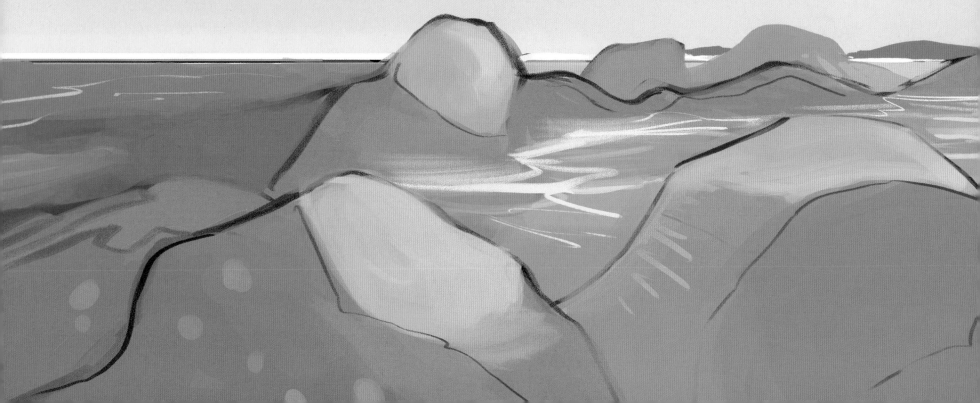

A giant rock there too.
I clamber up up up
shivers in my tummy,
pause,
then plug my nose
and slippety-slide
under the glossy blue.

"Kenzie!"
Mermaid Kenzie.
Mama head for our blue-bottom boat,
Josefina Dos,
seabirds crooning an about-to-sail-off song.

I wiggle into my mermaid tail,
grab my spear and net,
and we set sail.

We read the ocean
like other folk study books.

I look for seabirds and turtles
and dolphins and whales and
my seal buddy, Cocoa,
snout smooth as sea glass,
spiraling through waves with her zip zoomy tail.

Mama puts on her snorkel and mask.
Bubble cheeks, then
we sink into the water chute,
past a school of silvery fish
wafting in shafts of filtered light,
sea fans swaying.
My coils wave too
inside the deepening darkening blue.

The shipwreck
rests on the sandy floor;
littered with bottles and netting and trash.
I kick my tail into a swarm of moon jellies—no—plastic bags!

Backstroking, heart beat beat beating in my ear,
I can't believe it.
More plastic bags than fish!

"When I was a girl, the sea was an underwater zoo," Mama say.

"Octopus. Jellyfish. Fingerlings. Krill.

Squishy squashy sea creatures."

What can I do?

"The ocean is a promise," Mama say.

"It's broken now." I sigh. "Look!
Will these plastic bits end up in the bellies of my friends like Cocoa?"
I search the waves for my freckle-faced chum.
And the seabirds and turtles
and dolphins and whales.
"It ends up inside us, too," Mama say.

"The ocean is turning into plastic stew," I sing.
"O, my friends, what shall we do?"

I grab my spear and mermaid net
and scoop what junk I can.

"But *you* said mermaids don't clean up," Mama say.

"Higgledy-piggledy," I say. "*This* mermaid cleans up for my sea pals."

"I am proud for you," Mama say, eyes twinkling.

Back on the shimmery shore,
I spot trash everywhere.
"Beach Do-Up Day," I declare.

Then I whip my tail and swing my net.
"We'll help," some new friends roar.

"I am Mermaid Kenzie,
Protector of the Deeps," I sing.
Then spike plastic bags and straws and cups.

Until the glittery lip of the sea is clean.

PLASTIC IN OUR OCEANS

When I was a girl growing up in the Pacific Northwest, I loved to eyeball whales—tuxedoed orcas, sleek, pearlescent belugas. As a grown-up, when I saw photographs of beached whales, bellies swollen with pounds and pounds of plastic waste, I was horrified. Other sea creatures have also been found stuffed with garbage: albatross, who normally devour colorful crustaceans, gulp checkers and markers, buttons and beads; sea turtles swallow shopping bags instead of jellyfish. Where is all this trash coming from?

When sea captain Charles Moore sailed from Honolulu back to Los Angeles in 1997, he didn't know he would cruise into a plastic stew in the Pacific Ocean. This monstrous dump of floating trash in the middle of the sea is now called the Great Pacific Garbage Patch. The earth has only one ocean, but five ocean basins: Pacific, Atlantic, Indian, Arctic, and Antarctic; and sadly, most of them have their own garbage patch.

I was shocked to learn the garbage includes everything from rubber ducks, Ping-Pong balls, and dolls to flip-flops, glue sticks, and diapers.

Oceans are downhill from everywhere, so plastic scoots, floats, and sails down to the deeps. Plastic is so lightweight that wind plucks it from trash cans, garbage trucks, and landfills and blows it out to sea. Then, the plastic breaks down into tiny bits, and ends up in the bellies of our water-living friends. Even if we don't litter and live hundreds of miles from the sea, our plastic stuff can still wind up in the ocean, so it is important for us to use as little plastic as we can.

Globally, 100,000 marine mammals die every year as a result of plastic pollution they either eat or get tangled up inside, like plastic-based fishing gear. This includes whales, dolphins, porpoises, seals, and sea lions.

What would you do if everyone was trashing your home and there was so much garbage you couldn't breathe? Superheroes around the world asked themselves that question on behalf of ocean creatures and got to work:

Nineteen-year-old Joshua Caraway, from Atlanta, Georgia, in the United States, grabbed a pair of gloves and some trash bags and began picking up litter on Miami Beach, Florida, instead of hanging out and listening to music during spring break. "I just love the environment and to clean up the earth," he said when his story went viral on social media in 2019.

Twelve-year-old Ralyn Satidtanasarn, aka Lilly, glides through canals in Bangkok, Thailand, on a paddleboard picking up cans, bags, and bottles in her war against plastic pollution. She convinced a major supermarket to stop giving out plastic bags one day per week and now other stores have pledged to stop handing out single-use plastic bags.

Afroz Shah organized a weekly beach cleanup in Mumbai, India, and educated his neighbors on the dangers of plastic pollution until it became the largest beach cleanup in history, clearing away eleven million pounds of trash. The beach became so clean that wildlife, like baby turtles, returned.

Dutch inventor Boyan Slat first dreamed of cleaning up the oceans while diving in Greece when he was sixteen. By the time he was eighteen, he founded The Ocean Cleanup and designed the first ocean plastic cleanup system—a floating barrier that collects plastic using only ocean currents. He is working on cleaning up rivers, too.

James Wakibia, a Kenyan photographer, started a social media campaign calling for a ban on plastics, especially plastic bags. By sharing his photos and writing enough letters to the editor, newspaper articles, and social media posts, he started a movement that succeeded in getting the entire country of Kenya to ban plastic bags.

#ReduceYourUse—People all over the world are pledging to reduce their use of plastic. I stopped using plastic water bottles to help save our ocean friends. **What will you *do*?**

BIBLIOGRAPHY

Moore, Charles and Cassandra Phillips. *Plastic Ocean: How a Sea Captain's Chance Discovery Launched a Determined Quest to Save the Oceans.* New York: Avery, 2011.

And for Younger Readers

The Mess That We Made, by Michelle Lord, illustrated by Julia Blattman. Brooklyn: Flashlight Press, 2020.

One Plastic Bag: Isatou Ceesay and the Recycling Women of the Gambia, by Miranda Paul, illustrated by Elizabeth Zunon. Minneapolis: Millbrook Press, 2015.

Plastic, Ahoy!: Investigating the Great Pacific Garbage Patch, by Patricia Newman, photographs by Annie Crawley. Minneapolis: Millbrook Press, 2014.

To my grandmermaids, Maya and Ella, and all protectors of the deeps —CWS

ACKNOWLEDGMENTS

The publisher and artist thank Millie Liu for her invaluable help in the final stages of the art.